"Christmas 2020"

A Mouse and a Miracle

By Cathy Gilmore

Illustrated by Jean Schoonover-Egolf

Cathy Gilmore

Tiny Virtue Heroes™ Book 1: Team JOY
A Mouse and a Miracle

Copyright © 2020 Virtue Incarnate. All rights reserved. No part of this book may be reproduced by any means without the written permission of the author and/or publisher.

First Edition: July 2020
ISBN 978-1-73349-353-6

Thank you! Each purchase of a Tiny Virtue Heroes™ book helps fund virtue literacy.

We believe that it is powerful to do small things in a big way. A portion of the sale of each Tiny Virtue Heroes™ book is donated to the virtue literacy efforts of Virtue Works Media. **Whenever your family or your school buys a book, you are supporting this important cause.** *Together, we can make virtue-nutrition available to spiritually at-risk and morally-impoverished children and families everywhere. Thank you so much!*

𝒫erpetual
𝓛ight
𝒫ublishing
www.perpetuallightpublishing.com

Visit www.VirtueHeroes.com
to know more.

Long ago, in a place called Israel, lived a humble girl who was a helper in the Jewish temple. She was so pretty, and nice, even to **mice** like me!

The girl loved God so much that kindness flowed from her heart to everyone, and in all she did.

She was one of a group of girls who helped at the temple. They dreamed about being chosen by God to be the mother of the MESSIAH, the King and Savior of all.

One girl longed to be a royal mommy. "I would love holding and rocking my baby, the King."

"I'd look so beautiful in my sparkling crown!" said another, imagining herself wearing royal jewels.

A third girl pictured a chest full of coins. "As the Queen Mother I could buy anything. And I could share some with the poor."

But the special girl talked about the goodness of the Messiah and not so much about herself.

She said,
"Your Holy One will come to save all the people. He will be our King forever!"

Perhaps you know who the girl is, but do you know me?

My name is Moshe. (You say it: "Mo-SHAY.") But you can call me Mo. I'm a mouse. I might be SMALL but I have a BIG story to tell you about that special girl.

She is my friend.

She's my **HERO!**

Her name is Mary!

Mary and I met at the temple.

We spent our days praying, weaving, baking, sweeping, and preparing for ceremonies to worship God.

We worked very hard. When evening came, we were all exhausted.

But Mary seemed fine.

Her prayer and hope in God seemed to give her more **strength.**

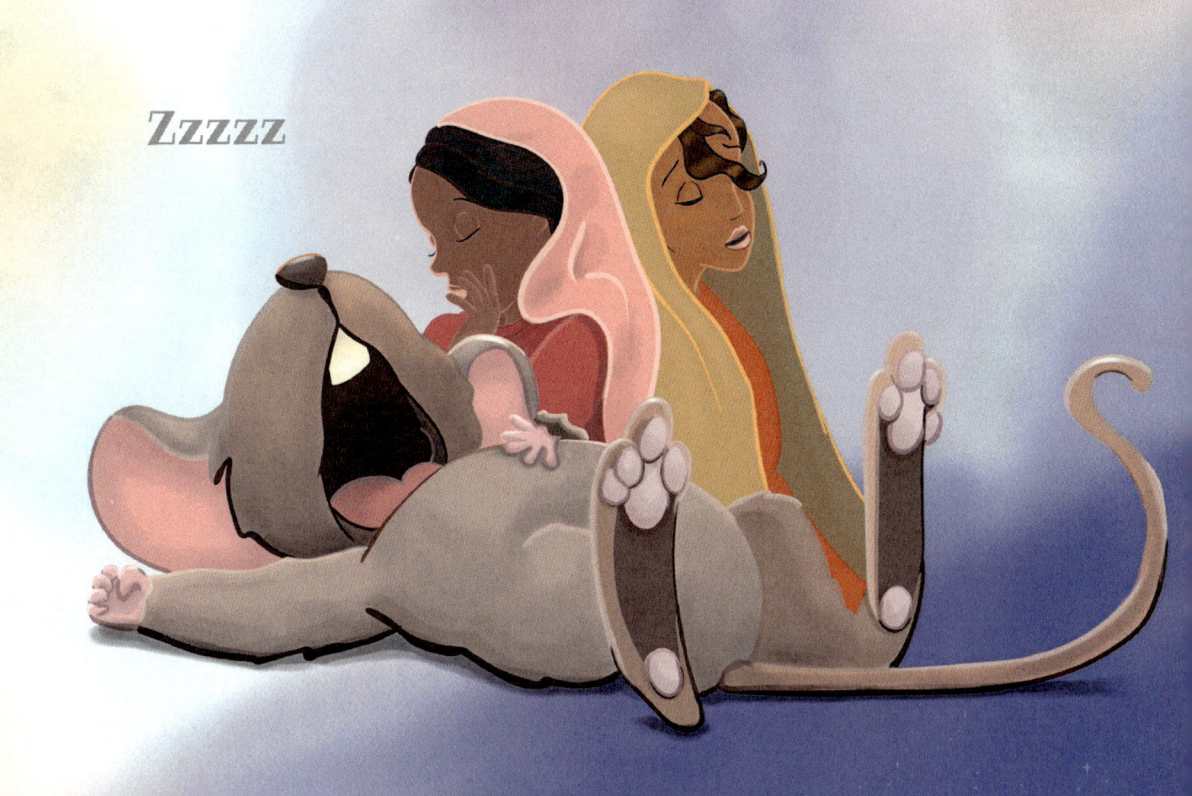

Zzzzz

One evening in the moonlight, she pretended to curtsey before a queen.

I could hear her whisper.

"I'd be so happy serving the royal mother and Child. I don't need to be big or important."

"My joy would be to **serve** in the court of the Messiah King, as a handmaiden to His holy Queen Mother."

But around Mary's fourteenth birthday, BIG CHANGES began.

Joseph the carpenter, who was a great-great-great-grandson of King David, was chosen by God to be Mary's husband.

Mary was troubled.

She said, "I planned to give my whole life to God serving as a handmaiden in His Church."

Mary's mother Anna comforted her. She said, "Be at peace. This, too, is God's will. You will be a **Holy Family.**"

Mary quietly accepted God's plans.

When she returned to her hometown, Mary took me with her. In Nazareth, I stayed with her as she happily hummed, worked, and prayed through each day.

Sometimes, she would softly thank God for always caring for His people in the past.

She unrolled a little scroll. "God, You saved the Israelites, my people, through a poor little baby named Moses. Will You save us again soon?"

Mary would talk to ANGELS, too.

Everyone has a guardian angel. Many people ask them for help sometimes. Mary seemed to have a whole team of them!

She spoke to them like they were her best **friends,** though I didn't see anything.

I just heard quiet, happy, and peaceful conversations.

Then one day, as she was praying, it happened.

I *did* see something.

An angel appeared and said,

"HAIL, full of grace! The Lord is with you. Blessed are you among women."

Startled by such a ROYAL greeting, Mary wondered what the angel meant.

"Fear not, Mary, for you were chosen by God. You shall conceive and bear a Son. His name will be **JESUS**. As the Son of the Most High, His kingdom will have no end."

Trembling, yet smiling, Mary asked, "How shall all this come to be?"

The angel answered,

"The Holy Spirit shall come upon you, and the power of God shall overshadow you.

"The Holy One shall be called the SON OF GOD."

Everything Mary had sung and prayed about was coming true!

Except she wasn't going to be a servant to the Messiah's mother.

God was asking her to *be* the Messiah's mother!

Mary said,

"I am the HANDMAID of the Lord.
Be it done to me as you say."

At that moment, Mary became the mother of the Messiah.

All of her ancestors had been waiting HUNDREDS and hundreds of years for this **promise** to be fulfilled.

And a tiny mouse like me got to see it happen! I knew she was a hero!

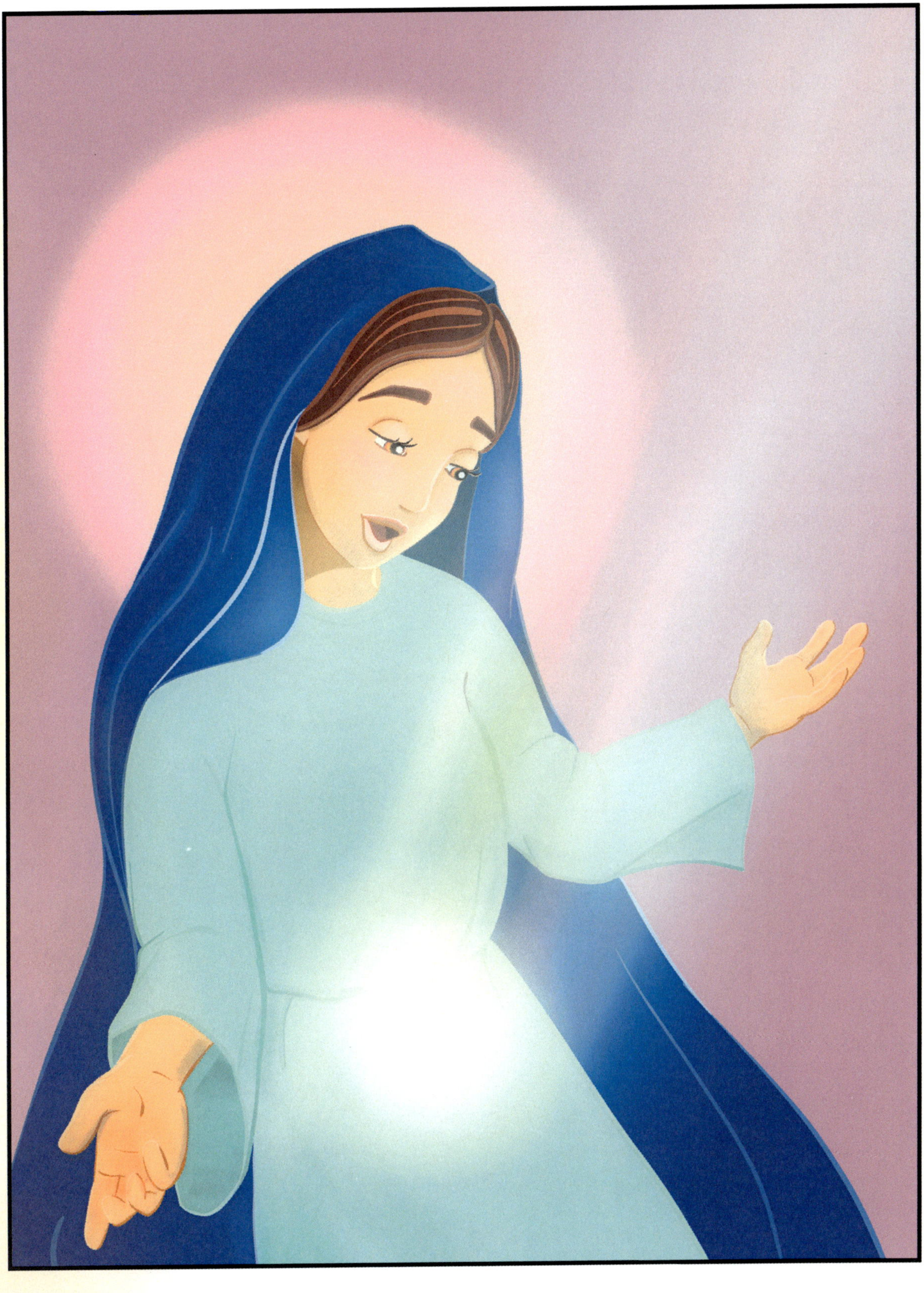

Then the angel left her. Everything looked as it was before.

All except Mary.

If anyone ever looked full of GRACE, it was Mary on that day. She glowed with a simple goodness inside and out.

She wasn't just any hero. She was a *virtue hero* of **humility.**

With God's grace, her littleness was a BIG strength.

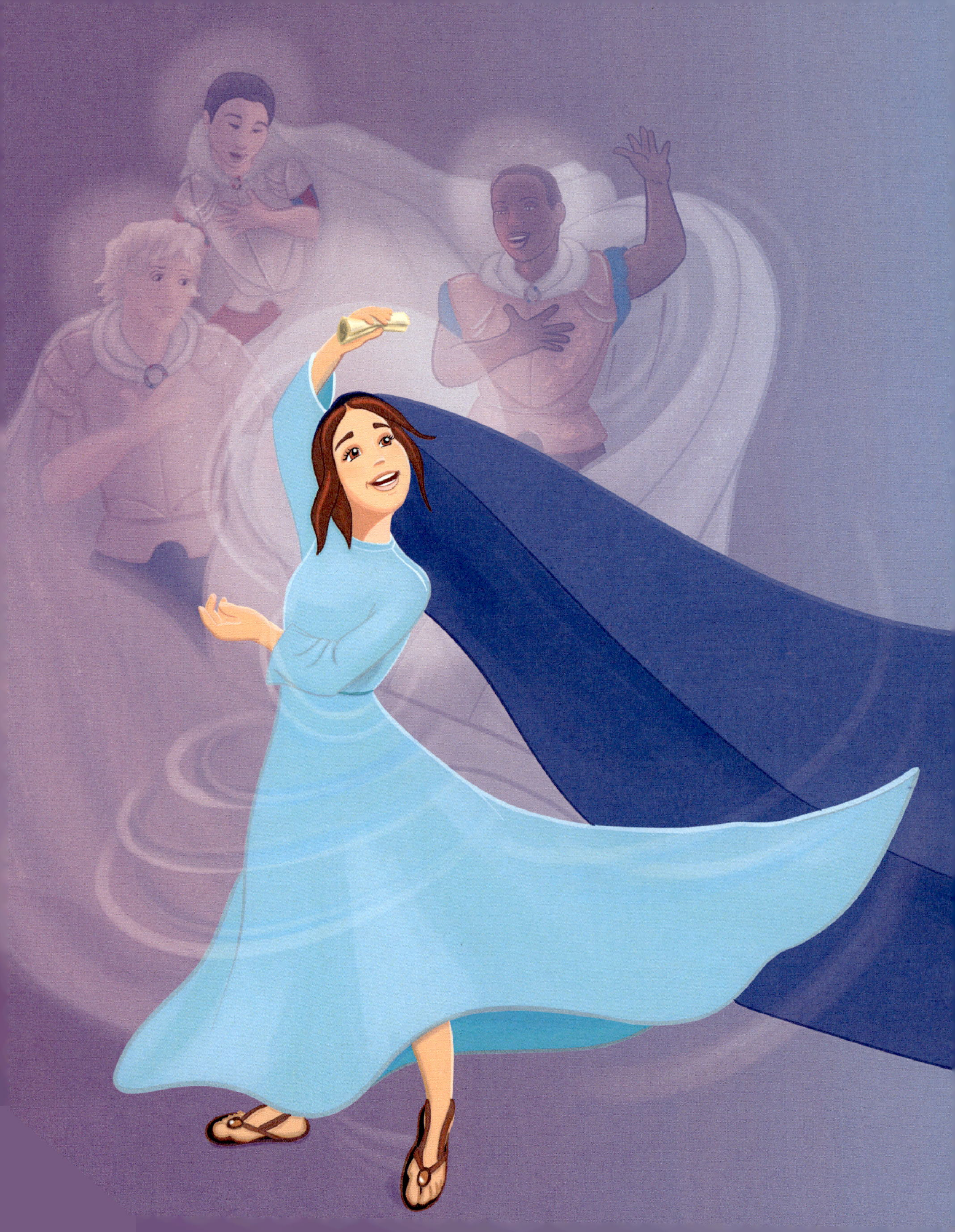

Mary twirled around and danced with JOY!

She said, "Praised are You, God, my King! Your love blesses everything!"

And just for a moment, I could see the angels dancing with us.

Hi Readers!

I'm a Tiny Virtue Hero, a storyteller, a sidekick, and your friend. You can think of me as your play-time or pray-time partner. I tell everyone the virtue story of my hero Mary, mother of Jesus the Messiah.

Mary is my hero because she shows me that there is strength in being humble and small. Mary isn't just *any* hero. She is a **virtue** hero of HUMILITY.

VIRTUES

are the power of God's goodness alive in us. Prayer makes us VIRTUE STRONG.

Pray a prayer with me:

Dear God, our Father, Your Son became a tiny little one to save us all. Help me to be a Virtue Hero, like humble Mary, even though I am small.

You can be a VIRTUE HERO!

When we ask God to guide what we **think** and **pray**, **do** and **say**, we enable holy habits like HUMILITY to grow virtue-strong in us.

Mary shows us that staying close to God and to our guardian angels powers up our virtue strength, and enables us to be Virtue Heroes™!

MOSHE
CHARACTER CARD

Virtue Power: HUMILITY, choosing the strength of littleness

Virtue Color: YELLOW

Tiny Virtue Hero Team: TEAM JOY

Favorite Story: The Annunciation, when Mary said YES to being the mother of Jesus

Favorite BIBLE VIRTUE HERO: Mary (Jesus's mom) as a girl

Favorite MISSION VIRTUE HERO: Justo Takayama Ukon, from Japan

Mo invites us to pray in a special way for the MISSION VIRTUE Region of: ASIA

MISSION VIRTUE HERO:
Justo Takayama Ukon

Justo Takayama Ukon is a Mission Virtue Hero. As a humble hero of holiness, he lived most of his life as a Samurai warrior in Japan. That's a small nation located in the Mission Virtue Region of ASIA.

Justo had courageous humility. He had humble love for both friends and enemies. His humility ignited a love for Christ in many souls. Like me, he admired Mary's virtue strength.

You may feel as small as a mouse, but if you love God you can humbly offer to serve Him. God can make your life a BIG adventure like Justo Takayama Ukon. Because his life was so full of heroic virtue, he is now known as Blessed Justo Takayama Ukon.

Justo Takayama, "Kirishitan Samurai," traded his sword for the cross.

Justo Takayama Ukon, please pray for all of us to grow strong in the virtue of HUMILITY.

MISSION VIRTUE Prayer Power-UP
Mission Region: ASIA

We can be Mission Virtue Heroes in two ways. First, we can pray for people who live far away from us. Second, we can pray for people whose souls are far away from Jesus. Let's pray a BIG prayer today for the people with whom Justo Takayama Ukon lived and loved in the Land of the Rising Sun. Let's pray for everyone living in Japan and all of the Mission Virtue Region of ASIA. We can pray like this:

God, please bless everyone in ASIA: especially the poor people, the sick people, the sad people, and all of the missionaries who bring Jesus to them. Help all of us to grow in the virtue of HUMILITY.

Meet the creator of Tiny Virtue Heroes™: **Cathy Gilmore**

Author

An award-winning children's author, Cathy is an advocate for virtue. Known as "Mrs. Virtue Lady," Cathy is passionate about assisting parents, grandparents, and teachers to infuse every family with fervent faith and vibrant virtue. Her Tiny Virtue Heroes™ are a menagerie of animal and insect characters who gently model faith and morality. They invite readers of all ages to admire real-life virtue heroes from Christian history.

By energizing the imaginations of children via stories, Cathy is on a quest to place **virtue** at the heart of how kids think of super heroes and super powers. Find out about all the Virtue Heroes™, as well as Cathy's broader efforts to promote virtue, at her website www.VirtueHeroes.com.

Ministry Founder

Cathy is also the founder of Virtue Works Media, the 501c3 non-profit ministry that promotes **virtue literacy**: expanding the knowledge and practice of virtue in children, teens, and families through the experience of reading and media. Find out more about choosing morally "nutritious" content in books, films, and music by visiting www.VirtueWorks.Media.

Meet the Tiny Virtue Heroes™ Illustrator: **Jeanie Egolf**

Jeanie is the talented artist working to bring Cathy's Virtue Heroes™ characters and storybooks to life. Jeanie has a personal passion to create images that are emotionally engaging for children. Jeanie's style integrates a broad spectrum of skills in graphic design, fine art, and children's illustration enriching her ability to create unique and timeless characters. Discover more of Jeanie's work at: www.MollyMcBrideandthePurpleHabit.com

The Tiny Virtue Heroes™

Virtue	Name
HUMILITY	Moshe
INSPIRATION	Devoree
WISDOM	Amel
GRATITUDE	Ziva
KINDNESS	Eli
ADAPTABILITY	Petros
TRUST	Tito & Alba
CHARITY	Joktan
JOYFULNESS	Simcha
HONESTY	Chava
EMPATHY	Gavri
FORTITUDE	Tanton
INTEGRITY	Durie
PERSERVERENCE	Yadi
SELF-DISCIPLINE	Chucar
PEACEFULNESS	Palti
FAITH	Jakeem
HOPE	Tikva
MODESTY	Shira
DEVOTION	Parpar
HUMOR	Sal
FAITHFULNESS	Max
JUSTICE	Barb
COOPERATION	Lia
STEADFASTNESS	Shilo
COURAGE	Amasi
ACCEPTANCE	Melee
MERCY	Anyela
PATIENCE	Leon
PRUDENCE	Nuru
OBEDIENCE	Jun
RESOURCEFULNESS	Hahona
PURITY	Cara
RESPECT	Pipit
MODERATION	Wasa

To learn about all these Virtue Heroes™ visit www.VirtueHeroes.com.

Visit www.VirtueHeroes.com
to know more.

If you enjoyed this book, please be sure to leave a review at your favorite book-reviewing sites!

Perpetual Light Publishing
www.perpetuallightpublishing.com